Broken Spear

Ron Mueller

ೞ *Broken Spear* ೞ

By: *Ron Mueller*

Around the World Publishing LLC
Cincinnati, Ohio

Broken Spear ©

ISBN 13: 978-1-68223-411-2

Distributed by Ingram
Cover Design By: Ron Mueller
Cover Picture By: Hien Mueller

The Stories of Taelo are set in the distant past, long before the time currently given as to when people migrated into the western hemisphere.

This is purposely done since the stories are meant to engage the reader in a story and not relate exact history.

The adventures of Taelo and Golden Hawk provide the backdrop for stories featuring the values of treating others as you wish to be treated, of responsibility, integrity, honesty and of contribution, and the joy of learning

Ron Mueller

ℰℭ Dedicated to all those who are,
wise and accepting of differences, existing,
among and between each of us.

Ron Mueller

On the third sun cycle, he came to a crest overlooking a valley and could see an abundance of elk mixed with buffalo grazing on the tall grasses.

Long Spear assigned the members to their locations and then sent them out to create a large circle. He instructed them on how to handle the elk and the buffalo. Each animal would act differently but each would be trying to break out of the circle.

The action each hunter had to carry out was to spear the animal and then follow through with a strike to the side of the head with their stone headed clubs.

Once everyone was in position, Long Spear gave the signal to start closing the circle. The circle was slowly tightened until the animals realized they were surrounded. The buffalo herd seemed to sense the situation and moved in unison as they followed the lead buffalo.

Long Spear and two of his young hunters were able to bring down a young buffalo that was on the way past them.

Silver Arrow had similar success on his side of the herd.

Two other hunters successfully downed a large female elk. They were shouting and dancing around their kill.

Long Spear complimented the two hunters on their kill but pointed out that all twelve of them had contributed equally. It had been their cooperation that had led them to a successful first hunt encounter.

Two buffalo and one large elk was almost enough for the hunt team to return to their home camp.

Long Spear and Silver Arrow showed the team how to field dress the three animals. They were gutted and the desirable inner organs were put in the animal's chest cavity. They then had the animals pulled to the edge of the forest and hoisted into the trees.

Long Spear decide that the team would follow the herd and see if they could once again experience success. He asked the two hunters that had downed the elk to stay and keep predators away from the animals that had been killed. He rewarded them by leaving them each some salt and a tender tongue to roast.

The team caught up with the herd and was able to take down an additional buffalo.

Long Spear decided that three buffalo and an elk was enough for the team to pull back to their valley.

Four travois were needed for the return trip.

Now Long Spear felt good about having the large number young hunters with him.

He assigned two persons to each travois. The extra four persons would rotate into a pulling position every one-hundred spear throw lengths.

This would make sure each person got several periods of rest as they made their return. This would allow him to maintain a fast pace back to the village.